DRAWING B.C.

BEFORE COMPUTERS

DRAWING TECHNIQUES OF ILLUSTRATION'S GOLDEN AGE

Published by Island Press
310 E. First Street
Ocean Isle Beach NC 28469
www.millerpope.com

Cover and interior design: Miller Pope
Cover illustration: Miller Pope
Interior illustrations: Miller Pope

Printed in USA

LIBRARY OF CONGRESS CATALOGING-IN-PUBLICATION DATA

Pope, Miller.

Drawing B.C. © 2009 Miller Pope
Miller Pope; illustrated by the author.

ISBN 978-1-60743-751-2

AUTHORS NOTE

This book is dedicated to all those who love drawing and to those who are nostalgic for the magical years of radio drama, film noir, and short story publications.

The illustrations within were all created in that bygone period for story illustration, before television and computers reigned supreme. It was a time when short story magazines thrived.

Colliers, The Saturday Evening Post, Blue Book, Red Book, Saga, and many more have all faded away and the few that survive, such as *Cosmopolitan* and *Good Housekeeping*, are completely different magazines than their earlier incarnations.

A large portion of the art used for advertising and story illustration in the decades immediately following the Second World War was basic line drawings due to the high cost of color separation and reproduction. The art used in this book may not be the same size as the original publication.

I shall always be grateful for having been a participant in the field of illustration during those wonderful years.

Miller Pope

In my Westport, Connecticut studio circa 1959.

CONTENTS

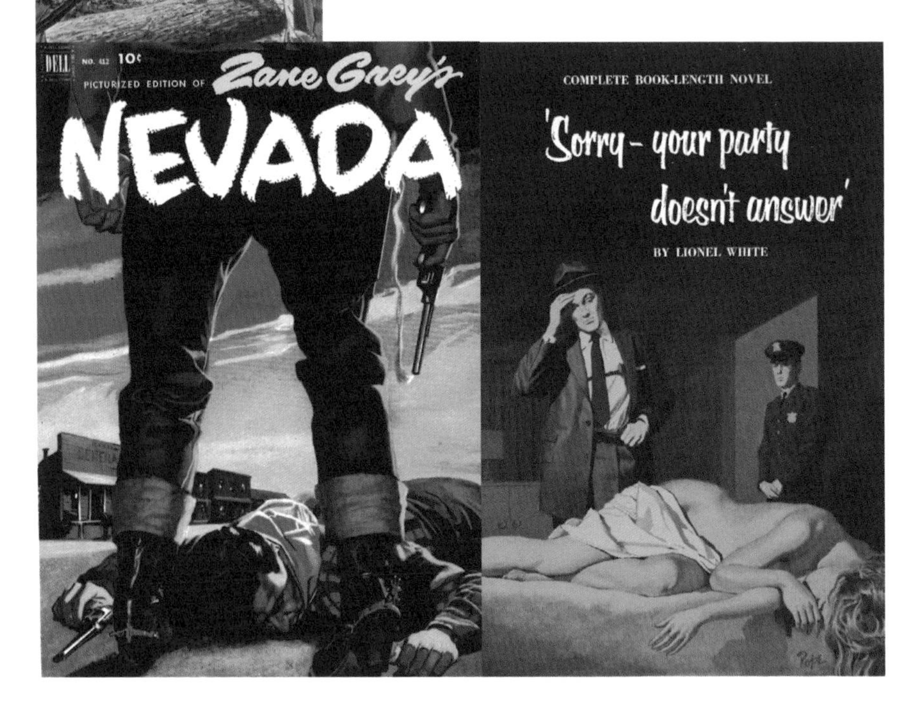

DELL
10¢
PICTURIZED EDITION OF
Zane Grey's
NEVADA
COMPLETE BOOK-LENGTH NOVEL
'Sorry - your party doesn't answer'
BY LIONEL WHITE

PREFACE

Since long before the dawn of recorded history, man has strived to depict three-dimensional things in simple two-dimensional line drawings. Examples of these drawings, dating back more than ten thousand years, have been preserved in the dark recesses of caves in France and Spain. Many of our primitive ancestors' depiction of animals possess a high degree of sophistication and realism, which is remarkable since they were done completely from memory in the dim light of a torch or simple oil flame.

In this age of computer technology, line drawing no longer occupies the large niche it once did. Color separation and printing is now far easier and less expensive than in times past. This has led to the partial demise of line drawing but it remains for many a high art form — a mastery of which can form the foundation of outstanding art.

Line art is nothing more than drawing in its simplest and basic form. The great masters of the past based their paintings on a foundation of solid draftsmanship.

The purpose of this book is not to teach anatomical drawing, but rather to supply some techniques for enhancing stand-alone line art as well as to provide some techniques for using line as the basis for other art forms. Many outstanding books on anatomical drawing, perspective, color, composition, and other subjects exist, so few basics will be covered in this book.

I have always strived for as much realism in my work as I could achieve, but many of the techniques espoused in this book will apply to non-realistic art as well. Art can be primitive, distorted, stylized, or almost anything, as long as it is not apologetic.

Pope

PENCIL

These drawings of little girls dressing up in their mother's clothes and the little girl in the zoo were done with an ordinary soft (#2) pencil on an illustration board with a very slight tooth.

PEN AND INK

Here are examples drawn in india ink with a pen and brush on ordinary smooth illustration board.

They were first drawn in pencil and after ink was applied, the pencil was removed with a soft eraser.

PRESS
MILLER POPE

PRISMACOLOR PENCIL

The illustrations shown were drawn with a black prismacolor pencil on ordinary illustration board to which a "tooth" had been added by an application of cassien white paint greatly diluted with water and then left to dry.

The black Prismacolor pencil produces solid blacks with a slightly softer edge than ink with either pen or brush.

CHARCOAL

A textured line that is hard and soft at the same time is rendered by a charcoal stick or a charcoal pencil. This is best used when the subject matter can be kept simple.

CHARCOAL AND INK

A charcoal stick or a charcoal pencil can be combined with ink or paint as in this drawing of astronaut Neil Armstrong.

FELT MARKER AND PASTEL

Felt markers mixed with pastel produce an interesting result. A smuge stick is useful for blending pastel and softening edges.

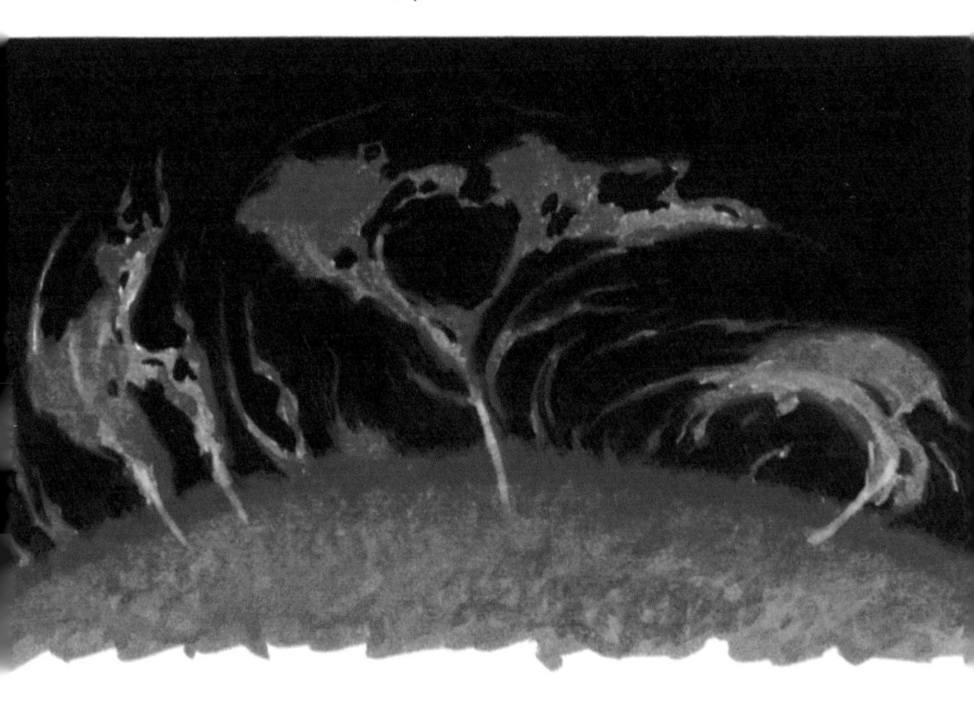

DRY BRUSH

This dry brush illustration shows the technique of applying the medium with a partially dry brush.

Old felt markers that are partially dry can also be used.

PASTEL

Pastel can be used to produce dramatic effects as in this illustration.

The blank space contained the story title and the first pages of text.

It also contributed to the sense of heighth and danger.

PASTEL AND INK

Pastel was combined with ink to produce this illustration.

Most of the drawing was done in pastel but a little India ink was used to highlight a few places like the eyes and the glasses.

Here again the blank space contained the story title and the first page of text.

VACANCY
6T02
XB165

MIXED MEDIA

This illustration is a combination of ink, pencil, and watercolor.
The artist should not be afraid to mix media.
Use whatever it takes to get the job done.

TEXTURED INK LINE

These examples demonstrate how the different treatment of lines can lead to a variety of effects.

Vive le différence!

COLOR PENCILS

This magazine cover looks like a painting but it's not. I did it entirely with colored pencils. It would have been easier to paint it but I was curious to see if it could be done with pencils. It was well received, but having proved to myself that it could be done, I went back to paint for future jobs of that type.

PENCIL WITH INK ACCENTS

A simple pencil drawing can be enhanced with the addition of a few India ink accents.

I did this during a period when I was experimenting with distortion.

LESS IS MORE

The great architect, Mies van der Rohe, described his philosophy of modern unadorned architectural design as "Less is more."

This principle should often be applied to line drawings.

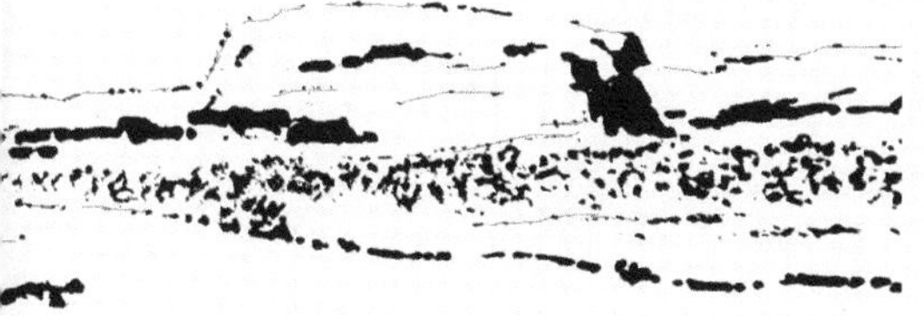

Unnecessary detail detracts the eye from the essentials of the composition.

LEAVE SOMETHING

TO THE IMAGINATION

Let the viewer be your partner and fill in part of your drawing.

PAINTING WITH LINE

I call this type of drawing, painting with line, when tones are simulated by solid blacks, solid whites, and strokes and cross hatching.

An India ink fountain pen was a great time saver for this kind of drawing.

Do not put India ink in an ordinary fountain pen. It will clog up and ruin the pen!

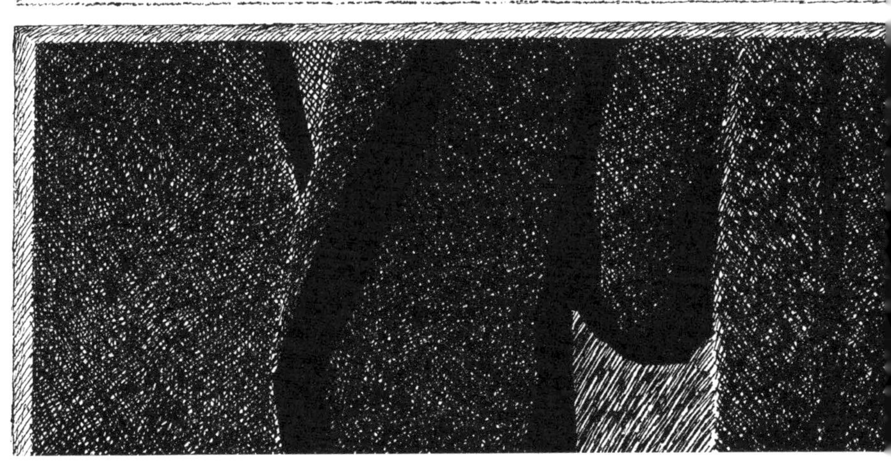

REST THE EYE

A drawing can have a lot of detail without becoming too "busy."

Resist the urge to go overboard with detail and leave some solid whites and blacks to rest the eye of the viewer.

LINE WITH FLAT COLOR

Before the days of Photoshop and automatic color separation, two-color separation was usually done by the artist with the use of an overlay of film or paper.

The overlay was always executed in black or red but the printed color was the second color that was designated by the publication.

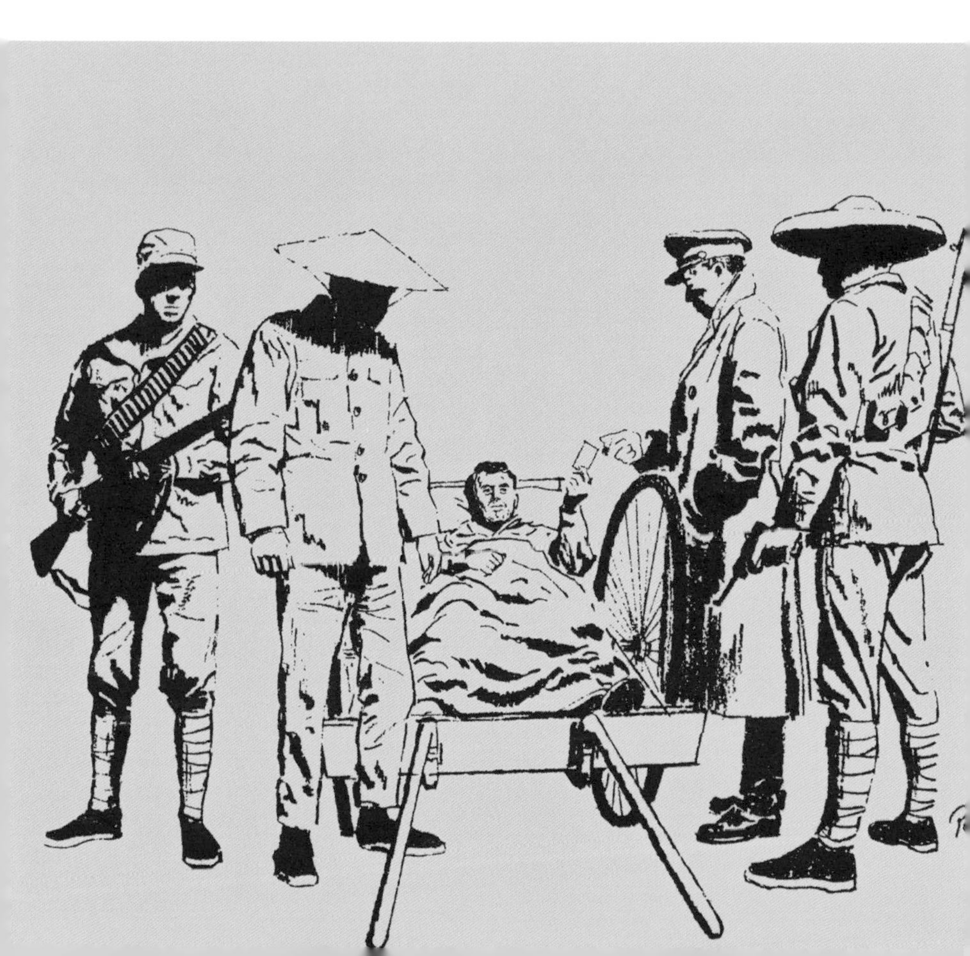

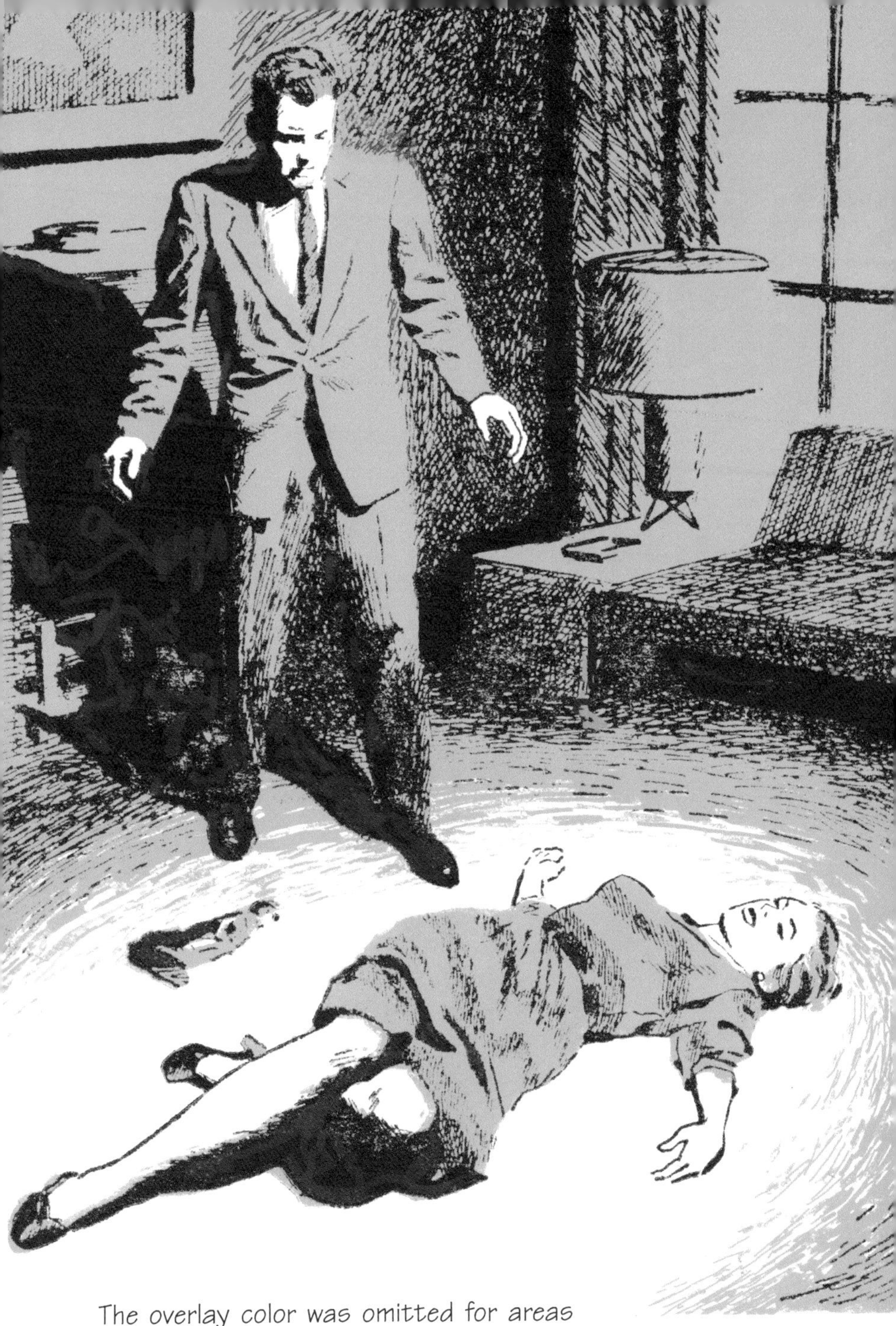

The overlay color was omitted for areas of white or the color of paper the drawing was printed on.

INK, FLAT COLOR, INK WASH, AND SMUDGED PENCIL

Thc shouting woman was drawn in pen and ink with a flat color overlay. The ball players were also executed in ink with an ink wash for the shadows and wrinkles and plain pencil smudged with a smudge stick around them.

INK, WATERCOLOR AND SMUDGED PENCIL

India ink line with plain pencil smudged with a smudge stick provides the grays, and watercolor on an overlay supplies the color in this simple illustration.

TWO COLORS OF LINE

Interesting effects can be achieved by combining a black line drawing with a color overlay, which is another line drawing.

FEW LINES

These are examples of drawings where few lines are needed.

They consist of large areas of black and color.

HEAVY SHADOWS

Heavy shadows suggest darkness and menace.

The illustrator can cash in on the viewer's natural fear of darkness.

In these illustrations the shadows create drama and a feeling of danger.

LINE AND HALFTONE

The main figure in this illustration is executed in halftone India ink wash, and line is used to emphasize the fact that he is an automotive designer.

In this illustration the freighter is a halftone drawing and the map in line is used to emphasize that it is engaged in world trade.

GLAZED LINE

These illustrations were executed in line with a black Prismacolor pencil. A glaze consisting of a little opaque watercolor, Elmer's glue, and water, was washed over them.

When dry, some areas were painted out or muted in white.

Because Elmer's glue dries perfectly clear it can be used to give a unique effect. Colors can be suspended in it with very little mixing between.

PENCIL AND PAINT ON PREPARED BOARD

The figures were drawn in pencil and black Prismacolor pencil on an area painted in a yellowish color. Next colors were added with both watercolor and color pencils.

White paint was used to lighten, mute, and isolate areas of the drawing.

COLOR WITH WATER COLOR PENCIL ON SMOOTH BOARD

The figures were drawn in black pencil on an area painted yellow. Next colors were added with both watercolor and color pencils.

Areas of the drawing were lightened and muted with white paint.

COLOR PENCILS

Examples shown were done entirely with color pencils.

OIL CRAYONS

Oil crayons are very different than the wax crayons used by children.

Their application is smoother and their colors are more vivid due to the much greater pigmentation they possess.

INK LINE AND FELT MARKERS

Felt markers offer an excellent and quick way to add color to a line drawing.

Color pencils can also be added to the mix if more texture is desired.

LINE WITH AN INK WASH

Quite often all that is needed for an effective result is a very simple ink wash, touch of watercolor, or other type of tone, to make an effective statement.

Brauhaus

INK WASH

An ink wash is a simple way to add tone and detail to a line drawing by applying a transparent mixture of water and India ink to the drawing.

The more ink in the mixture the darker the tone.

Wash drawings were once very common.

LINE ON TEXTURED PAPER

This illustration gets its texture from having been drawn on textured paper.

Different paper texture produces different line texture.

FACES

The noses of pretty girls should often be de-emphasized; the teeth of both men and women should not be defined except for the elderly and for evil characters. Unnecessary details in the faces of beautiful women should be avoided.

Exaggerated eyelashes often contribute to feminine beauty.

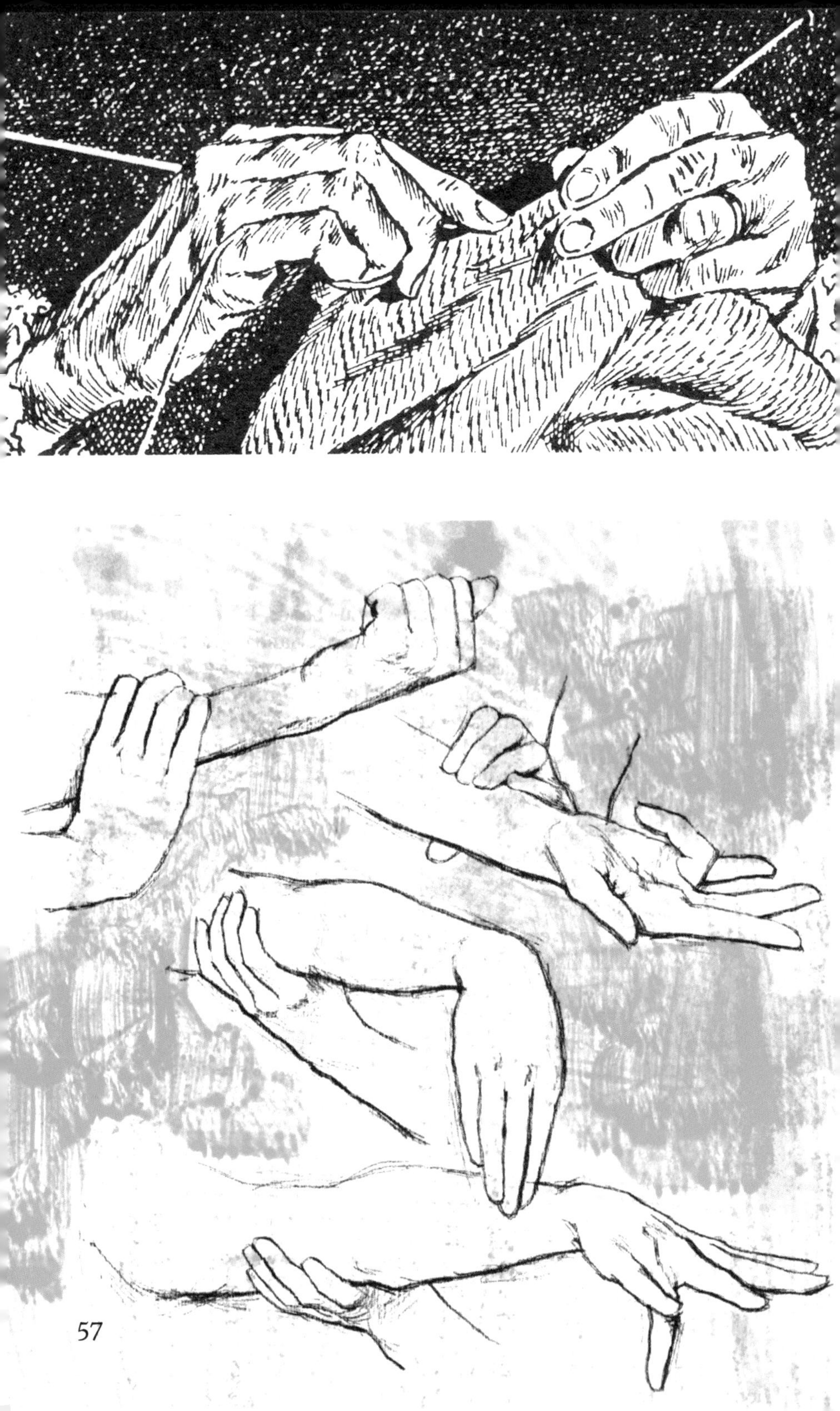

Hands should be drawn with "authority," emphasizing angles. The knuckles should be well defined and details such as fingernails should most often be de-emphasized except when the hands are large or when they are those of a very old person.

Extra details detract the eye from the essentials.

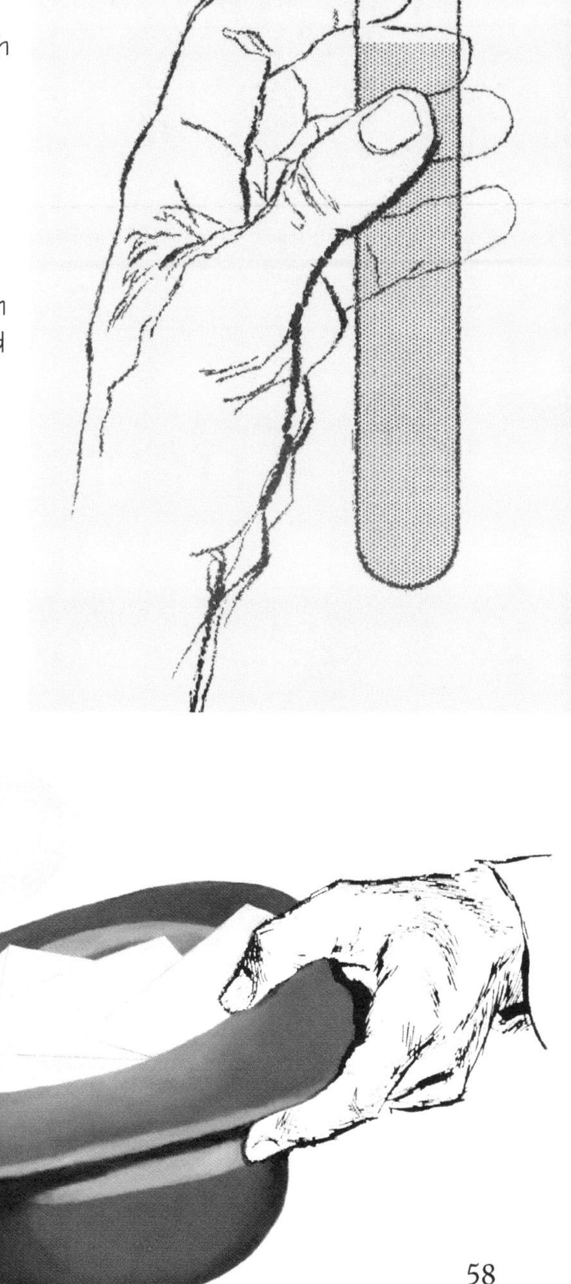

LINE OVER TONE OR COLOR

Line drawings can be created over a swatch or other shape of halftone or color. The effect is much the same as doing things in reverse.

LINE AND FLAT TONE

Line drawings mixed with flat shapes of halftone or color often creates an interesting effect.

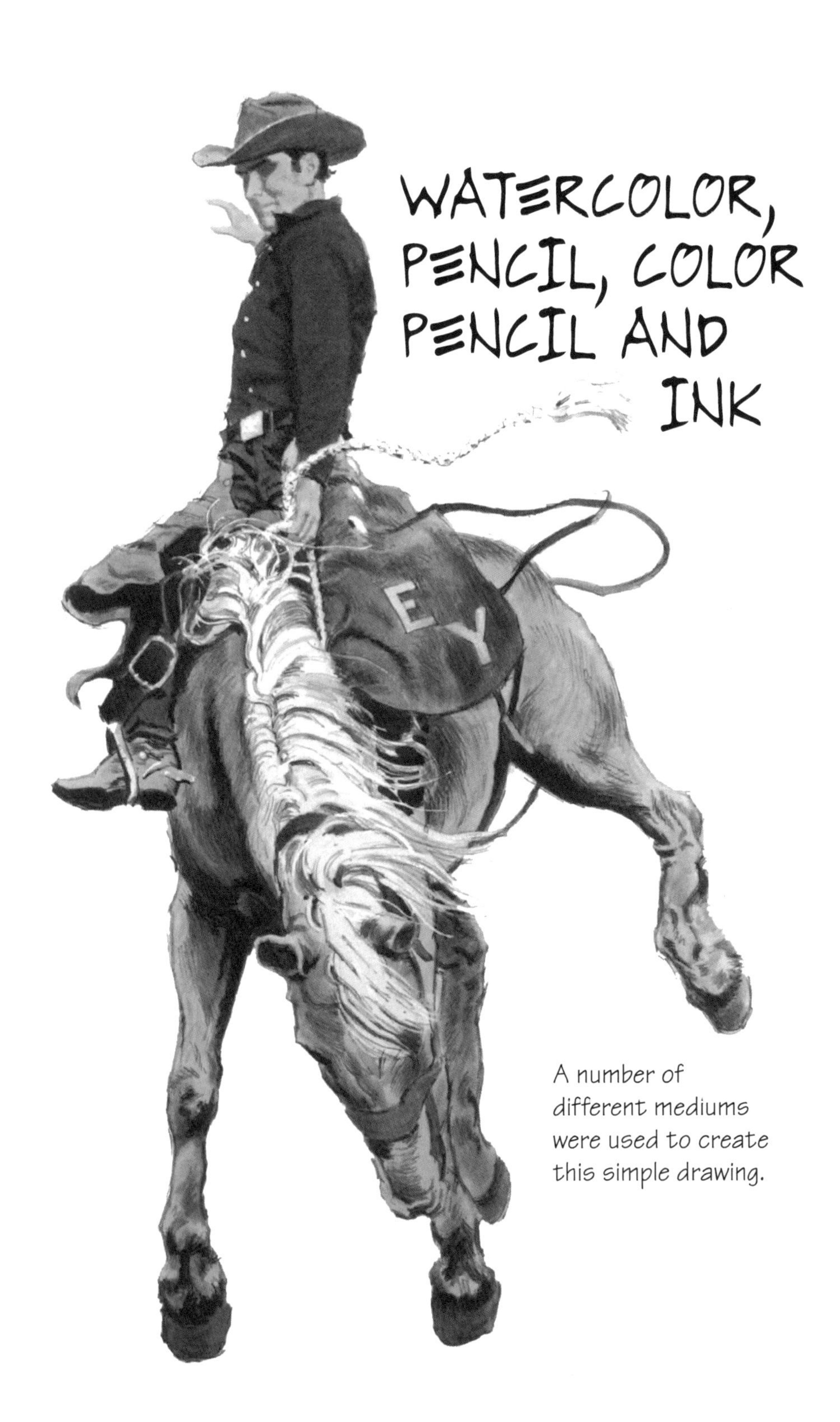

WATERCOLOR, PENCIL, COLOR PENCIL AND INK

A number of different mediums were used to create this simple drawing.

OPAQUE WATERCOLOR

Opaque watercolor is a form of drawing because it dries rapidly making it difficult to blend colors as with other painting mediums. Blends are largely achieved by dry brushing and close values.

LINE, COLOR PENCIL, AND WATERCOLOR ON A PAINTED BACKGROUND

These examples were created with black line drawings over a painted background with the addition of watercolor and color pencils.

Some areas were then muted or painted out with white paint.

LINE ON COLORED PAPER

Cut out shapes of color paper were pasted down and a line drawing was added over the paper.

I only did this once. It was too much work.

GLOSSARY OF MEDIA USED IN THIS BOOK

The drawings in this book were done in the nineteen fifties and sixties but most or all the media used is still available.

Shown in this photo is a bottle of India ink, a bottle of Elmer's glue, smudge sticks, a black Prismacolor pencil, #2 pencils, and various erasers.

The wad of rubber in the center is a soft kneaded eraser. It can be molded into an infinite number of shapes.

A smudge stick consists of tightly rolled paper that can be cut to a point or angle. It is used to soften and blend pastel and charcoal.